SMELLY BILL

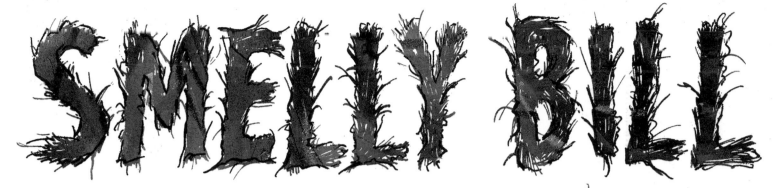

STINKS AGAIN

Daniel Postgate

meadowside
CHILDREN'S BOOKS

Bill loved to
climb in rubbish bins
And so he smelt of many things,
And I can tell you none of those
Was very pleasant on the nose.

Bill was clever, tricky, tough,
And nobody was smart enough
To get that rascal in the tub
And give his fur a soapy scrub.

Nobody, except for one...

There was only one who could,
A legend in the neighbourhood.

Her name was...

...GREAT
AUNT BLEACH,
and she,

Was every stinkers'
enemy.

One day Bill's folks went on a trip
And Bleach came round to doggie-sit.

Bill heard the rubber gloves go 'SNAP'...

"It's scrubber-dubber time,
    dear chap!"

Up the garden path Bill fled,
And jumped onto the garden shed.
With bark and growl and howl and yelp
He called around the town for help.

OOOOOWWW!

From far and wide,
in leaps and bounds,
There came Bill's band of loyal hounds.
A shocking bunch of filthy freaks
Who hadn't had a bath in weeks.

Stagnant Stan, who stank of cheese
And was a happy home for fleas.

Putrid Pete, a creature who
Just loved to roll in his own pooh.

Filthy Fred, his favourite dish?
It was a bag of rotting fish.

And **Rancid** Ron, with pong so strong
That they could smell him in Hong Kong.

In a whirl of fur and fleas,
They dashed around Aunt Bleach,
Snapping at her heels and knees,
Which made the old girl screech:

"Please don't bite me, please don't eat me,
Go inside you'll see
My shopping bag's filled to the brim
With sausages and chicken wings
And lots of other yummy things
Much tastier than me!"

In they ran, each greedy mut
Expecting something lovely but
Instead they found four ladies who,
With hair of purple, pink and blue,
Were waiting for them

with shampoo!

Bill's flea-bag bunch turned tail to make
A desperate effort to escape.
But no! Bleach blocked their way completely.

"Bathtime, boys,"

she told them sweetly.

Then dogs and aunties went to war,
Fighting bravely,
tooth and claw...

Auntie Florence grappled Stan.
Round and round the room
they span.

Putrid Pete fought
Aunt Jemima,
Watch out for the
priceless china!

Rancid Ron and Auntie Glynn
both determined they would win.

Filthy Fred on Auntie Dee...
Now that was quite
a sight to see!

The dogs fought till they could no more,
Then fell exhausted on the floor.
The aunties all let out a roar

And danced around

victorious...

...Triumphant,
proud and glorious!

Then they took those filthy pets
Slowly up the creaking steps,
Up to where no dog would dare
To dream of in his worst nightmare.

When they came home, Bill's family
Were really quite surprised to see
Not one clean dog...

...but five no less!

Shame the house was such a **mess!**

For all at
Westmeads Community Infant School,
in Whitstable

First published in 2007
by Meadowside Children's Books
185 Fleet Street
London EC4A 2HS
www.meadowsidebooks.com

A CIP catalogue record for this book
is available from the British Library
10 9 8 7 6 5 4 3 2 1
Printed in China